TOLD BY STARLIGHT
IN CHAD

Joseph Brahim Seid

Translated by Karen Haire Hoenig

Africa World Press, Inc.

P.O. Box 1892
Trenton, NJ 08607

P.O. Box 48
Asmara, ERITREA

Africa World Press, Inc.

P.O. Box 1892
Trenton, NJ 08607

P.O. Box 48
Asmara, ERITREA

Cover design: Saverance Publishing Services
Book design: Dapo Ojo-Ade

Seid, Joseph Brahim.
  [Au Tchad sous les étoiles. English]
  Told by starlight in Chad / Joseph Brahim Seid ; translated by Karen Haire Hoenig.
      p. cm.
  ISBN 1-59221-047-3 (cloth) -- ISBN 1-59221-048-1 (pbk.)
  1. Tales--Chad. 2. Chad--Folklore. I. Title.

GR355.5.S45 2007
398.2096743--dc22
                              2007003857

To my kind and gentle Grandmother
Who cradled my happy childhood
May God cover her with the
Glistening clouds of His mercy!

Contents

Translator's Acknowledgements and Notes

Thanks to:
- Peter Connor for his translation class and Fiona Siang Yun, my class-mate. Their input at the early stage of the translation was invaluable.
- Kofi Anyidoho and my dissertation committee for encouraging me to complete the translation and submit it for publication.
- Mary Hudson who shared her translation expertise and enthusiasm for the project.
- Madame Nabia-Seid who kindly provided biographic information on her father, and the U.S. Embassy at N'Djamena, Marissa Maurer and Felix Mbatalbaye who facilitated communications with Madame Seid.
- Angela Ajayi and Africa World Press, for the pleasure of working with them, and for choosing one of my father's photographs for the cover.

"les vivants constituent les maillons d'une chaîne qui re lie ceu qui ne sont plus à ceux qui naîtront. Les morts sont le sel de la terre, les vivants en goûtent la saveur"(the living are links in a chain, a chain connecting those who have gone before with those who are yet to be born. The dead are the salt of the earth, the living taste that salt). Joseph Brahim Seid, *Un Enfant du Tchad*, p.63.

I dedicate this translation to my father, John Norman Haire, who laid the foundation early with his infectious love for language and fascination with words. He became acquainted with the creative works of Joseph Brahim Seid during a stint of lecturing at the University of N'Djamena in 1979, and in fact had almost finished translating *Au Tchad sous les étoiles*. After his passing in 1995 we were unable to find the manuscript of his translation, but we do remember his appropriate title, *Told by Starlight in Chad*.

I have endeavored to bring the same meticulous care to the task that my father always brought to translation work. I can honestly say that I have enjoyed every minute of translating these stories, which attests surely to the quality of the original—Joseph Brahim Seid's simple and dignified storytelling style is, for me, the genius of this delightful collection.

Karen Haire Hoenig
Potchefstroom, April 2006

PREFACE

The Republic of Chad owes its name to a large lake, its blue and slightly salty waters dotted with papyrus plants. The northern territory of former French Equatorial Africa, it borders Libya, Sudan, Nigeria, former French West Africa and Cameroon. They say Chad is the land of sand and gold, but to tell the truth, its stretches of sand in turn give way to a savannah, composed of bushes, groves, acacia forests, tamarinds and baobabs...the habitat of many different species of fauna.

When the rains return, nature grows green again, as if transformed by the wave of a magic wand. The bush is drenched in vegetation; grass overruns the earth cloaking it in an emerald mantle, embroidered with wild flowers. The whole country becomes a vast paradise. Birds don all their colors and the air vibrates with their melodious song. This exuberance of life reminds man that once a year he must devote himself to the labors of the fields. Above all, it reminds him of divine omniscience. The sky covers over with large, dark clouds, which assume peculiar and grotesque shapes full of celestial humor! Lightning zigzags in flashing streaks. Nature, in a fury, rumbles and howls.... And the storm hurls a relentless voice down onto the shaken earth. Has God taken refuge here?

The dry season, in turn, has its picturesque quality. The air is sultry. The sun shines brilliantly in a very clear, very blue sky. Slowly, the earth dies. The grass turns yellow. The insects, from the little green locust with its gauze wings to the big praying mantis with its strong mandibles, flee from their hot hiding places. The worries of the drought are forgotten in the joys of the harvest. In every hut, the granary fills up with millet, corn, groundnuts and sesame seed.... Inhabitants of the same village share the produce of their labor. Each one gives away the greater portion of his harvest, but receives, with the other hand, more than he has given to his neighbors and friends. On important festivals, kith and kin come together for a copious feast. Tasty dishes await the guests. Custom dictates that whether they feel hungry or not, they eat a little food before wishing everyone the gift of grace, forgiveness and blessing.

In the evening, there are traditional games. Excitement fills the air; a tumult is unleashed. The drums reverberate, roar, summon to the dance. Their staccato boom echoes through the savannah and over the rolling, sandy hills. The young perform war dances, competing in strength, agility and skill. Simulating combat, they brandish their assegais, crouch, rise up and face off in rapid succession. They stamp the ground furiously with their feet: a cloud of dust envelops them in a tremendous halo of glory. All this time, the tom-toms are vibrating, their frenzy marvelously matching the dancers' movements. Rhythm of life, captivating, lyrical, spellbinding magic! With fertile, protean imagination, griot and bard recite the prowess and deeds of their distant ancestors or sing of the beauty and charms of their betrothed.

During all these seasons, the children of Chad are the happiest under the sun. When they are not working in the fields, they roam all over the bush picking wild fruits; armed with their assegais, they hunt guinea fowl, hare, porcupine and gazelle. One of their favorite pastimes, to this day, is to lie in wait for the teals and moorhens in pools strewn with water lilies. They are passionately fond of the large gatherings after nightfall, when the elders recount the most beautiful tales, which sometimes never end and must be resumed evening after evening under the light of the moon.

On behalf of these countless children of Chad, I invite you, dear reader, to come and sit among us, under a blue sky strewn with stars, to listen to these stories and legends, which tell of marvels and wonders. We ask only one thing: that you share in the joy of our candor and our innocence.

CHAD, LAND OF PLENTY, LAND OF HAPPINESS AND LAND OF BROTHERLY LOVE

A long, long time ago, so long that not one among us could say how many moons have since waxed and waned, a cataclysm sent by God shattered the earth. The earth was full of violence because, as we well know, men had acquired the knowledge of evil, and woe to them and their offspring. God looked on the earth and behold it was corrupt!

At that time, the skies did not cease from their scolding rumble. God, the Eternal, sent a ghastly rain of fire upon the earth. Everything was consumed. Only one tribe, Alifa's, was spared, most certainly sheltered by the mighty hand of the Eternal.

Alifa's tribe fled in terror, the shadow of divine mercy guarding and guiding their faltering steps. Alifa and his people fled without resting or sleeping, all the while singing praises to the Most High:

Lord, Lord,
Source of all life,
Creator, yourself not created
Yesterday as today,

In peace as in adversity,
You are the immoveable pillar.
We lean on you.
In faith and in hope,
Grant us a beautiful and tranquil death...

As the tribe approached, rivers and seas parted their tumultuous waters. Alifa and his people continued their flight, without drinking or eating, and all the while singing praises to the Most High. Even the hills and the highest mountains retreated into the bosom of mother earth. No sooner had the tribe passed than everything caved in behind them, as if swallowed up forever in an unfathomable, gaping abyss.

At long last, one evening, the skies ceased their rumbling and the fire stopped spreading all at once; gradually the ground became firm underfoot. At that calm and reflective hour when twilight descends, the tribe discovered the grassy banks of a large lake. There they stopped to gaze at a marvelous sight: little incandescent balls of fire, rising from the surface of the peaceful waters, drifted up into the sky, illuminating all of nature around.

Filled with wonder, Alifa and his people sang praises to the Eternal, for a long, long time, so long that each, exhausted, fell into a deep, peaceful sleep.

On awaking the following day, an even more astonishing sight greeted them: a giant in a giant pirogue on the waters of the large lake, fishing with nothing but his bare hands. Sometimes, as if at play, he would take hold of a hippopotamus by the ears, then delicately, though with quite a bit of splashing, drop him back into the water.

Seeing the tribe at prayer, he caught a huge fish and with the ease of a child throwing a stone, flung it to the bank. Alifa and his people leaned over the fish and for a long time gave thanks to the Eternal. When at length they stood up, the giant had disappeared. Now it was that for the first time in many, many days they assuaged their hunger.

That same evening, the giant reappeared and with the same remarkable dexterity threw them large earthen jars of delicately scented honey. The following day he returned to the bank with more earthen jars, this time filled with fresh milk, and invited Alifa to accompany him. Trusting in the ways of God, his Guardian, Alifa took his place next to the giant in the huge vessel. The pirogue moved swiftly, soon vanishing on the horizon, though the giant used nothing but his two big hands for oars.

On the far bank of the large lake, the chief of the tribe found a city with numerous gigantic huts. On reaching land, Alifa saw children as tall as palm trees in the nearby streets, sharing their games with lions, panthers, and rhinoceros. Huge snakes with luminous green eyes, slithering around their limbs, played a curious game of hide-and-seek with them.

On the trees of colossal girth, dense with foliage, countless birds were singing as they flew hither and thither. The air was vibrant with their mellifluous music.

Most blessed of lands! Here animals and people lived in the most perfect accord. Evil was unknown. Kindness reigned in every heart. Innocence shone in all eyes and no one was even aware of it. Work was revered. Strength, skill, intelligence and genius, everything which men receive at birth as a gift from God, was put to use for the common good: here to clear the forest which would soon give way to fertile fields, there to divert the course of rivers so as to irrigate the plantations, elsewhere to harness the lightning or the last rays of the setting sun so as to illuminate the city walls. And always, in all time and in all places to the greater glory of the Eternal.

Alifa was warmly received in this marvelous land. The people gathered round, eager to find out where he came from, who he was, what he knew. Alifa simply told them the story of his tribe and sang praises to the Most High:

Lord, Lord,
Source of all life,
Creator, yourself not created
Yesterday as today,
In peace as in adversity,
You are the immoveable pillar.
We lean on you.
In faith and in hope,
Grant us a beautiful and tranquil death...

When evening fell and Alifa asked to go back to his tribe, the giants persuaded him to stay and sent for his people. They made a noble gesture of hospitality; from now on this place would be their new home. As time passed, closer and closer relationships were formed with the giant people. Now it happened that some time later, a prince of the kindly giant people married a daughter of Alifa's tribe and the male child of this union became the ancestor of the Kotoko people. They called him Sao, which means harmony, love for all mankind.

And the large lake, which Alifa's tribe had discovered one evening at the calm and reflective hour, when twilight descends, was named Chad. Chad, land of plenty, land of happiness and land of brotherly love.

TWO

DJINGUE, OR THE FAMILY ASSEGAI

It came to pass a long, long time ago in a great kingdom on Lake Chad! Two sister tribes disputed the right of guardianship over an old family assegai called "Djingue," dedicated to the divinity and the worship of their shared ancestors.

A veritable civil war was about to break out and hurl the two groups against each other. This state of affairs did not inspire confidence among the young people of the country, whom each side wanted to arm in a war against their brothers and sisters. So the young people assembled and went to the representatives of their respective tribes, to persuade them to abandon their quarrel. The delegation was successful, but, not wanting to settle for a fleeting truce, they decided to dispose of this object of perpetual discord, once and for all.

Seizing the assegai, twelve exceedingly courageous young people set out one evening to carry the offending object far away. They trekked over mountains and through valleys, across the bush for seventy-seven days and seventy-seven nights. Along the way they fought boldly against nature, against wild beasts and against the inhabitants of the countries through which they passed.

Protected by the invigorating influx of the deity and by the strength of their departed ancestors, the twelve young people surmounted the obstacles, surprising and defeating the resistance of the peoples opposing their advance. They had entered every region armed, but with no thought of conquest. All they wanted was to find a vast expanse of land to call their own. At length, one evening they found themselves in the middle of a fertile and uninhabited valley. Their guide stopped. "Let us stay here," he said, "take possession of this land, and build our huts. Let us make this a sacred place, where our tribes can be united, henceforth bound together by our common origins."

Thereupon he drove the assegai into the earth under the shade of a tamarind tree and immediately set up a hut nearby. His companions did likewise. At first there was only a small village. Later, however, over the course of centuries, it became a large, flourishing and happy country, whose reputation spread for thousands of kilometers around.

In this way "Massenya," the capital of Bagirmi was founded and to this place all the races of the Lower and Middle Chari trace their most distant origins.

The names of the twelve young people who established this country are Dokko, father of the Sokoro, Birni Desse, Lubat Ko, Dukoat (known as Irro) Daboleni, Diongou, Djougueldou, Niouguonidoualla, Gougoum-Darko, Gougoum-Bida, Niougo-Kouboudga, Maguerba and NGolgargue.

They fathered twelve tribes which branched out into several lines. Among them one may still encounter today the Sokoros, the Bagirmians, the Kengas, the Bouas, the Bulalas, the Koukas, the Goulas, the Saraouas, and all the Saras: Mbaye, Dai, N'Gama, N'Gambaye....

And Djingue, the old family assegai, at the root of this flowering of the races, enjoys immense prestige to this day. Djingue, symbol of the great peace of man with the Divinity. Djingue, symbol of unity among men.

There is a Kenga saying that accurately defines the relations between these different groups: "The people of Massenya are just like us, the people of Fitri, of Lake Irro and the Saras are our brothers."

THREE

THE KINGDOM OF WADAI

In the twelfth year after the Flight (the year 632 according to our calendar), the prophet Mohammed died in Mecca. His mission was complete. Having succeeded in uniting the Arab world, he left his followers the clear charge of spreading Islam throughout the world.

After him came three caliphates. Those of Medina, chosen in the midst of raging rivalries, conquered Syria, the island of Cyprus, Egypt, Mesopotamia, Persia, Armenia and threatened Constantinople. Endless disagreements and internal struggles, however, engendered a crisis of faith, creating wide schisms in the fabric of the Muslim community. The believers were divided into "Sunnites" or orthodox Muslims, "Shi'ites" or supporters of Ali, the prophet's son-in-law, and "Kharijites" or dissidents.

Taking advantage of this split, Muawiyah founded the Umayyad dynasty which reigned for more than a hundred years and only came to an end with the assassination of Marwan II by Abu-al-Abbas. A golden age ensued, rendered illustrious by Al-Mansur and Harun-al-Rashid, the greatest and most liberal of the caliphs, whose memory lives on in the elegant and poetic legends of the *Thousand and One Nights.*

Despite its prosperity, however, this empire broke apart and was completely destroyed by the Turks. Thus the Baghdad caliphate disappeared forever.

The deposed Abbasid family took refuge in Egypt. One Abbasid, of whom history gives no account, fled to the Hijaz region and settled in Medina, where his son, Saleh, was born.

From an early age, the child was keen on learning. After completing his education, he made long excursions across Arabia and struck up friendships with the pilgrims who came from Black Africa. The pilgrims told him of the beauty of their lands and the noble qualities of their peoples: devotion to honor, hospitality and respect for the state of poverty when it is borne with fortitude and integrity. These things kindled Saleh's desire for adventure.

One day he followed the Black pilgrims to the edge of the Nile, continued to the interior, crossing Darfur and Dar Masalit, and finally reaching Wadai. There Saleh settled on a mountaintop and led the life of a marabou.

The presence of this recluse aroused the curiosity of the people living nearby, who sent a delegation of their wisest representatives to inquire what he was doing there. "I am carrying out my religious duties," replied Saleh. "I pray to Allah, who made heaven and earth, day and night, sun and moon, hot and cold, life and death...Allah watches over the destiny of the world!" Thereupon, he took the Koran, opened it, and reading the first verse, explained its meaning: "There is no god but Allah and Mohammed is his prophet! Allah wants us to adore him and pray to him each day!"

The messengers returned to the base of the mountain deep in thought. After hearing the delegates' account, the people of the country unanimously agreed to send for Saleh and from that time on, he lived among them, preaching Islam.

Some time later, when the faith had won over every heart, he was chosen as their religious leader and converted three tribes. Each tribe gave him a very pretty wife and in this manner, Saleh or Sileh, as the Wadaians call him, established the royal family to which every sultan of Wadai must belong.

Note: This Wadaian legend was mentioned by Carbou in his book *La Région du Tchad et du Ouaday*, volume II, pages 111 and following. Saleh or Sileh, the founder of Islam in Wadai, is also called Abd-al-Karim ben Djamé or Saleh ibn Abd Allah ibn Abbas. According to Carbou, he chased the Tunjurs from Wadai in 1700; according to Nachtigal he chased the Tunjurs from Wadai in 1635. In history, Wadai is also referred to as Dar Sileh.

FOUR

SULTAN SABUN

On a beautiful day in the dry season, a child was born in Sultan Gaudehn's household in Wara. The news flew from mouth to mouth, skipped from village to village, sounded from hilltop to hilltop and finally reached the kingdom's farthest bounds. The people of Wadai, men, women, young and old, rich and poor, hurried to Wara to honor the newborn child. Gold cascades, waves of silver, streams of emerald, beryl and precious stones poured into Wara. Sultan Gaudehn held a grand banquet. Several thousand guests celebrated this happy and joyous event. While young girls of amber and ebony complexion sang the praises of the young prince, numerous griots, each as distinguished as the next, composed marvelous verses. Day after day, night after night, the dancing continued. The atmosphere of gaiety and rejoicing only came to an end with the commencement of the naming ceremony. An assembly of fakihs, seers, witchdoctors and fetish doctors deliberated at length the name that should be given the newborn child. A happy compromise was reached: while a fakih wrote an amulet to put around the child's neck, a witchdoctor performed a frenzied dance to ward off the evil spirits and a fetish doctor combined several pulverized roots to produce a talisman with uncommon powers. The little prince was named Mahamat Abd-al-Karim, meaning the servant of God.

Just as the ceremony was drawing to a close, an elderly seer, his fingers adorned with copper rings, stepped out from a small group of bystanders and said to the assembly: "You have named him Mahamat Abd-al-Karim, but I give him the name Sabun, the Pure, in memory of our ancestors whose protecting shadows hover over Wara, because this child is destined for greatness!" Thereupon, he disappeared quietly into the crowd. And so it was that the young prince was called both Mahamat Abd-al-Karim and Sabun; but the name Sabun, more graceful, more gentle and more poetic, prevailed and was retained.

In the magnificent palace at Wara, Sabun enjoyed a happy and studious childhood. From an early age, the young prince was a keen scholar; by seventeen he had already completed his education.

As regards physique, Sabun was tall and handsome. He was energetic and of honest bearing. In various sporting contests he had no equal: when it came to wrestling, he was as strong as an ox, when it came to running, as swift as the wind, when it came to horsemanship, Sabun's skills were unrivalled and incomparable: he sought only the most restive and invincible horses.

As regards intellect, Sabun had grasped every science: he could divine the future by drawing symbols in the sand; he could read the beautiful Chadian sky like a large open book, pointing out each star by name and predicting the success or failure of the season, according to the position of each star. Over there is the polar star which shimmers in a golden halo and guides the traveler lost in the bush; over there, the Big Bear, which looks more like a giraffe lifting its head to graze in the branches of the tall trees because there is no grass left on the earth! Over here, a cluster of stars that resembles a hen gathering her chicks under her wings; this means there will be a good harvest this year, Chad will enjoy plenty....

All his learning and practical knowledge Sabun owed to men of renown: the wise fakih, Abd-el-Djelil, had taught him how to read and expound verses of the Koran; agid Adré Ngaré, the highly skilled warrior, had trained him for warfare; the philosopher, Aboul-Fedda, historian par excellence and poet in addition, had taught him all he knew; Dougous, the great witch-doctor, had initiated him into the secret of the occult sciences....

In short, young Sabun was both wise and knowledgeable. The man destined to bring eminence to Wadai!

One fine morning, the people of Wara were surprised to see the prince building a hut just like all the others in the village, far from his father's palace. Now the reason was this: for a long time Sultan Gaudehn had been losing interest in Sabun's mother. Once upon a time as beautiful as the swamp lily, she had lost her youthful charm. And so the sultan took his affections and attentions to another woman, the sweet and seductive Am-Birematte. He lavished her with riches and satisfied all her desires; he promoted her relatives to top positions in the country, entrusting to them the final say on important affairs of state. And as if this were not enough, Sultan Gaudehn listened to all the spiteful innuendoes it pleased Am-Birematte to make. And so it came about that he resolved to put Sabun's mother out of her royal dwelling. The people, it may be added, were greatly displeased. As for the young prince, he followed his mother, making his home far from the royal palace.

This gesture earned Sabun the respect and sympathy of all the subjects of the kingdom. Very quickly, the prince had a following of ardent admirers. The former dignitaries who had been removed from power took up his cause. Filled with anxiety, the new ruling class reacted immediately by urging Sultan Gaudehn to reprimand his son for want of obedience and filial respect. The sultan, however, paid no heed to their urgings. Encouraged by this attitude, Sabun's supporters henceforth began to oppose vehemently all those who owed fortune and social position to the mere fact of belonging to the family and tribe of Queen Am-Birematte. A revolt, if not a full-blown civil war, might have broken out, but by good fortune this outcome was averted.

One evening, just when it seemed that peace had been restored, a rumor spread agitation and anguish throughout the kingdom. It was said that Sultan Gaudehn was dying! At this news, the people assembled and betook themselves at once to the palace to prevent the Sultan's entourage from extracting a promise that would jeopardize prince Sabun's succession to the throne. Gaudehn passed away without being able to lay down his last will. And since it was customary in such a situation to choose a new Sultan straightaway, the people forced the chief dignitaries to proceed with Sabun's enthronement ceremony and the consecration rite without delay. Imam Chafardine, after having preached on the source of the powers and the legitimacy of princes, delivered into Sabun's hands the amulet of power, the warrior's saber and the book of wisdom, the Koran. These objects comprise the legacy passed down from sovereign to sovereign, without which no one can reign in Wadai. Only after the performance of these rites could the people prepare the funeral for the deceased sultan.

The next day, the burial drums resounded, followed by the tom-toms for happier days, announcing to the world that one reign had ended and another was beginning.

The accession of Sultan Sabun ushered in an era of prosperity and magnificence for the kingdom. The young monarch proved to be charitable and kind to the poor and needy, just and fair to the rich and powerful. His leadership could be summed up in the saying of the Prophet, which he had engraved on the front of the public buildings: "The pursuit of justice brings riches, the pursuit of injustice, ruin." Sabun was a model of integrity, energy and generosity for as long as he reigned in Wadai.

He turned his kingdom to good account, encouraging the

cultivation of crops, animal husbandry and skilled trades. He promoted commerce by opening up three main routes, linking Wadai with The Sudan, Libya and Egypt. He established amicable relations with all these countries: his cousin, Jaffar, was his representative to the viceroy in Cairo, Mehemet Ali; his ambassador, abbo Naçour, one of the most astute diplomats of the day, entered into favorable treaties with King Senoussi of Tripoli and the Mahdi of Khordofan.

Sabun opened schools everywhere and turned the Abecher mosque into the intellectual capital of the world. In its day, it was the seat of human learning, excelling in the arts and humanities.

During his reign, Wadai was known the world over. People came to buy livestock, gum arabic and gold dust.... People came as well from the most diverse and distant horizons to learn at the feet of the most brilliant teachers, from whom one could never tell which ray of universal truth might be shed on the most perplexing problems of philosophy, ethics, religion and theodicy. Never had Wadai reached such heights.

The prosperity and happiness of the Wadaians must have attracted the envy of neighboring kingdoms and for several decades Sabun's reign unfolded in the midst of bloody wars. Sultan Abd-al-Rahaman of Bagirmi and Sultan Terab of Darfur threatened Wadai. Sabun faced the former first, raising an army and attacking Abd-al-Rahaman on his own territory. A fierce battle brought the armies face to face in Bougmine, close to Massenya. Day and night, for weeks on end, the bush knew no other sounds than exploding gunfire, neighing horses falling in battle, the groans of the dying and the cry of warriors exhorting their companions to fight. The Bagirmian army only found safety in headlong retreat. Massenya was declared a free city and Sultan Abd-al-Rahaman surrendered unconditionally. Sabun imposed his suzerainty and made Bagirmi tributary to Wadai.

Later, he launched his army against Darfur. King Terab's

army was formidable: strong, brave, fearless and irreproachable. Nevertheless, Sabun attacked him at Kabkabiyya. A terrible man-to-man battle ensued, the warriors on both sides fighting like lions. Rivers of blood covered the earth in a scarlet cloak. Despite their courage and tenacity, the enemy soldiers could not avert defeat and death. Sultan Terab fell right in the middle of the battle, his death now deciding the fate of the two armies. Sabun carried off the victory of a hard-fought struggle. So much blood was spilled in this place that even today nothing will grow here.

Freed henceforth from the anxieties of war, Sultan Sabun devoted himself exclusively to the good governance of Wadai. It soon became the metropolis of Central Africa. His administration suppressed debauchery and improper morals and was ruthless with those guilty of violent crimes. He ensured safety on the roads and the physical protection of persons and property to such an extent that a woman could leave her jewelry on the main road and find it again the next day exactly where she had left it. Order emerged everywhere and peace prevailed in the towns and in the countryside.

During his sultanate, Sabun had seen three generations grow up. His hair had turned white, his face was lined with wrinkles, but although old and succumbing to weariness, he still exerted himself in the service of his people. His willpower and sense of duty to his office were such that his collapse was sudden. On the first day of the month of Rahmadan, the holy month of peace and rest, death, which always comes without warning, knocked at his door; the good Sultan passed away peacefully. It was a sad and difficult day for the people of Wadai. A heavy silence hung in the air, which was normally gay; nature itself seemed to announce to the world that something great had disappeared! All at once, the breeze ceased, the spurges and thorns on the dust paths stopped quivering and the birds fell silent in the foliage. The sky assumed a lifeless hue and covered over with large, pallid clouds.

The death of Sultan Sabun was like his birth, but instead of joy, sadness and grief weighed on every heart. Waves of people from the surrounding countryside and from distant lands surged towards Wara. The sultan of Bagirmi, the caliph of Kanem, the sheiks of Salamat came to blend their tears with those of the Wadaians. Kings, princes, vassals and subjects mourned for the man who had given Wadai its strength, vitality, magnificence and repute.

The funereal ceremony lasted several days, in an atmosphere suffused with mingling aromatic perfumes: incense, myrrh and aloe.

Sabun was buried in the cemetery at Wara next to his ancestor, Sultan Saleh or Sileh, the Abbasid. Today his grave is simply a little mound of golden sand, shaded by a climbing evergreen plant. A place of pilgrimage and reflection. May Allah, the Merciful, protect the soul of Sultan Sabun, the exemplary Muslim prince.

Note: Mahamat Gaudehn, Sabun's father, is the descendant of Saleh or Sileh. He is the sixth descendant of the first Abd-al-Karim. Sabun is the seventh. He reigned from around 1785 to 1815. According to the history of Bagirmi, Sabun came to punish Sultan Abd-al-Rahaman Gaourang for his misconduct and corruption (1785-1806).

FIVE

BIDI-CAMOUN, TCHOUROMA'S HORSE

A very long time ago, in the days when miracles and wonders were still common among us, a little prince was born in the kingdom of Lake Fitri. Tchouroma was his name; noone knew the reason why. His father loved him dearly and his mother adored him. At a very young age, they had given him as a gift Bidi-Camoun, a splendid chestnut horse. When Tchouroma had barely reached his fifteenth year, his gentle mother died, snatched away by a cruel disease in her chest, which neither the skill of the fakihs, the fetish doctors nor the Bulala witchdoctors could cure. In memory of his beloved wife, the Sultan retained a great affection for the child. He took him lion hunting and on walks around the lake which is the sanctuary of the ancestral spirits and the safeguard of the kingdom. Devoured with envy by the King's great fondness for his son, the women of the harem devised plots to kill the child. One day they baked some poisonous cakes for him. Just as the prince was about to bite into one of the cakes, he heard his horse neighing in a most extraordinary way. Running to his horse, he found the animal with an anguished expression, his nostrils streaming with perspiration. For a long time the horse merely raised and lowered his head, refusing to acknowledge the little prince's consoling pats on the neck. Then, mystery of mysteries, he whispered: "Noble master, eat nothing but what your father eats, drink nothing but what your father drinks; accept none of the delicacies prepared by the hand of the women of the harem, for everything they serve you is poisoned. Be careful!"

At first, Tchouroma was struck dumb but he quickly composed himself, and returning to the palace, he declined the cakes. For several weeks the wicked women tried ruse after ruse to bring down the little prince, but since nothing worked they began to wonder if someone were not betraying them. One evening the enigma was revealed. One of the women heard the horse whispering to his master: "Noble master, eat nothing but what your father eats, drink nothing but what your father drinks." Thereupon, the woman ran to her companions to tell them what she had just heard. They held counsel and there and then decided to kill the horse. To carry out this plan, they summoned the country's greatest witchdoctor, who, in return for a handsome fee, suggested that one of the women should pretend to be ill. Then, as soon as the king called for him, he would advise him to kill Tchouroma's horse.

Finding this an ingenious scheme, the wicked women applauded their success. The following day one of the women pretended to be ill and took to her bed for several days. The king was anxious and called for the witchdoctor, who counseled him: "Oh King, a powerful and envious spirit bears a grudge against your house. To regain the favor of the gods you must sacrifice Tchouroma's horse." The King made no objection and a day was set for the sacrificial ceremony. That same day, returning from a hunting expedition, the little prince found his horse in a miserable state. The animal whispered: "Dear master, I am ruined. The women of the harem have succeeded in their pernicious scheme. Your father has resolved to have me sacrificed to save the life of the woman who deliberately took to her bed a few days ago." A lump came to Tchouroma's throat. He fell on the horse's neck, covering him with tears and kisses. Touched by this show of affection, Bidi-Camoun said to his master: "Wipe your tears, Tchouroma. Trust me. The day before I am to be executed you will ask your father to let you perform your equestrian skills one last time and we will be saved."

The young prince nodded in agreement, then betook himself to the palace where his father informed him of Bidi-Camoun's imminent death. Tchouroma let no sign of displeasure show, but requested his father's permission to ride his horse one last time before it was to be slaughtered. The king granted the favor, and so, when the day of sacrifice arrived, everyone knew that the little prince was going to perform some equestrian feats on his horse. The tom-toms were droning and the young girls of the kingdom were singing Tchouroma's praise.

Tchouroma appeared, dressed in raiments of gold, and Bidi-Camoun was splendidly harnessed. Mounting his horse in the midst of thunderous applause, Tchouroma performed two rounds of equestrian feats. So magnificent was the performance that mouths dropped open in admiration for the young rider. During the last feat, miracle of miracles, the horse took off into the air. A loud shriek of astonishment mixed with terror broke from the crowd. Bidi-Camoun rose high into the clouds, so high that he soon vanished from sight.

He came to rest a great distance away on the outskirts of a kingdom a thousand times larger than Fitri. The horse and his master, exhausted after such a long journey through the sky, fell into a deep, restful sleep. When they awoke, Bidi-Camoun said to the young prince: "the time has come to make your way in life, Tchouroma. King Dongo who reigns in this kingdom is much more powerful than your father. He has a daughter of exquisite beauty and in a few days he is going to offer her hand in marriage to the suitor of her choosing. So leave me in this place; I have the power to make myself invisible; disguise yourself as a poor man and go to the palace to seek work. You will have no regrets. I will support you in this time of trial and as a pledge of my fidelity, here are a few hairs from my mane; each time you need me, simply burn one and I will be at you side immediately. Farewell, dear master."

Taking off his raiments of gold and his sword of silver, the little prince entrusted them to his horse and set out in rags for King Dongo's palace, where he was taken on as a gardener.

Every day Tchouroma performed his work conscientiously, turning the soil, raking the soil, hoeing the soil and weeding the soil.... One evening, overcome with fatigue, he sat down for a moment on the edge of the well. Glancing up at the royal palace, he caught sight of a delightful young woman, standing at one of the windows. It was the princess, Aicha, who was contemplating the garden. Tresses of luscious silky hair fell enchantingly about her shoulders. To attract her attention, Tchouroma took out one of the horsehairs and burned it. In an instant Bidi-Camoun was at his side. The young prince dressed in haste and performed a spectacular display of horsemanship for the young woman. The enchanting display stole the princess' heart, but she told no one. The young prince, changing into his rags, went back to work.

Some time later, King Dongo summoned all the dignitaries and men of repute in the kingdom. He announced that his daughter was to choose from their ranks a husband. The young princess appeared and solemnly declared that her choice of husband was Tchouroma, the gardener. A cry erupted from the crowd. Indignant, the king flew into a rage and invited his daughter to retract her words. But as the princess would not, he chased her from the palace. In like manner he expelled Tchouroma. Left without food or shelter, the sweethearts took refuge with Zirega, the old sorceress.

A few days after these events, King Dongo fell ill and no one could cure him. Zirega, the sorceress, was consulted only as a last resort. She predicted a speedy recovery for the King and prescribed a calabash of fresh milk drawn from a doe which had just given birth. Immediately the King ordered his subjects to scour the bush and bring him back the healing milk. On Zirega's advice, Tchouroma went to the palace and asked the ailing king for a horse so that he might follow the others. He received a poor welcome from Dongo, who, to be rid of him, gave him a pitiful old horse, plagued with all the infirmities that can possibly afflict an animal. His name was "last-legs." Without a word, Tchouroma set off, limping along on "last-legs." Once outside the village, he tied the old horse to a tree, summoned Bidi-Camoun, and galloped off with the speed of lightning. For a long time, he crossed the bush without meeting a single doe. Finally, exhausted, he rested for a moment under the generous shade of a tamarind tree and dozed off. In a sort of reverie, he heard the old sorceress: "Get up and take a look," she told him; "I have gathered all the does in the savannah. Fill your gourd with the healing milk!" Tchouroma opened his eyes and saw, as if by magic, countless animals of all sizes and colors, peaceably jostling and pressing against one another at his feet. One doe, of her own accord, filled Tchouroma's container with her milk. Just at this moment the King's subjects appeared. The young prince drew his sword: "What do you want?" he asked. "Sire," they replied, "we have come on behalf of His Majesty, who is ill, to ask for a little of the doe's milk." "I will not give you any of this remedy until each of you has received a slash on the back of the neck at my sword," replied Tchouroma. "Such are the orders of the spirit of the bush who has made me guardian of the animals."

King Dongo's subjects bent down to receive the slash on the back of the neck from Tchouroma's sword. After this, he let them draw milk from the unsuitable does, and sent them away. Tchouroma followed them at a distance and re-entered the village, limping along on "last-legs." He paid no heed to the contemptuous laughter that greeted him at the palace, but went straight to the

King and held out his gourd. The King drank the contents with contempt, but was nevertheless cured instantaneously. This deed was worthy of a reward but Dongo gave none.

Several months later, a war broke out. Plunderers swept through the kingdom and the inhabitants were compelled to take up arms. Tchouroma took his place on "last-legs" among King Dongo's soldiers. The battle was fierce and the plunderers seemed to have the upper hand. Tchouroma again summoned Bidi-Camoun and with his sword cut off a few thousand enemy heads. Panic-stricken, the plunderers retreated in confusion. A great and resounding victory went down in the annals of the kingdom. But peace was far from being restored. The enemy returned, this time stronger than before and the fighting resumed. Tchouroma fought in a river of blood. This time, the victory was decisive. Re-entering his capital, King Dongo was welcomed with a volley of applause and shouts of joy. Filled with pride and glory, all the combatants performed wonderful equestrian displays for their lady friends. Tchouroma did some caracoles on "last-legs" for Aicha who was awaiting him. As for the crowd, however, they received him with exasperating jeers.

The next day, the king assembled his people and asked that the valiant warrior, whose conduct had been so fearless, so irreproachable, make himself known. Some liars stepped forward, but Dongo sent them back to their places, saying: "The valiant young warrior looked nothing like any of you!" At that moment Zirega, the sorceress, arrived: "Your Excellency," she said, "the valiant warrior you are looking for resides at my house."

The King summoned him and when Tchouroma appeared a long silence greeted him. The young man looked the king and his dignitaries in the eye and spoke with dignity: "King Dongo, you have made me the laughing stock of all your subjects. My conduct, however, has been exemplary. You were ill and I cured you; your kingdom was threatened and I saved it. Am I still unworthy of princess Aicha's hand? Know this, King Dongo, that the noble blood of Sultan Djurab-al-Fil who reigns on the banks of Lake Fitri, runs through my veins." Having spoken these words, Tchouroma called Bidi-Camoun and in less than a moment became the valiant warrior who had sown terror and death among the enemy ranks. Everyone applauded. King Dongo asked his forgiveness, then arranged for the marriage of Princess Aicha and Prince Tchouroma to be celebrated in pomp and magnificence. A delegation was sent to the Bulala Sultan to bring him to his son's wedding. For four entire moons, there was dancing to strains of the flute and the lute. Celebrated bards from every corner of the kingdom sang immortal poems in honor of the newly-weds.

The young couple showered the old sorceress with kindness throughout her life and Bidi-Camoun became the ancestor of the country's sturdy, swift steeds. His mysterious shadow continues to haunt the imagination of the Bulala warriors, who, in the face of adversity, misfortune and calamity still expect from their faithful mounts a miracle, which never happens.

SIX

THE MAGIC CAP, PURSE AND CANE

The events of this story took place three times two thousand years ago. On the banks of the Chari lived a rich young ship owner named Liman. He enjoyed considerable influence and a good reputation. In fact, many of the tribes living along the river had asked to come under his suzerainty. There was, however, a great rivalry between Liman and the sultan of Goulfei, who reigned on the left bank of the Chari. This rivalry might have lasted a very long time indeed had not Providence decided otherwise.

The sultan of Goulfei had a daughter of incomparable beauty. As gentle and delicate as a flower in the season of the rains, she was the talk of the entire country. Everywhere, in the streets, in the village square, at the market, in fishing and hunting parties alike, the young men talked of nothing but princess Gada's looks and lines. Each one secretly cherished the hope of one day making his fortune so that he might go and ask her hand in marriage. Liman, however, left nothing to fate. Having attained fortune and fame, he went to request her hand in marriage. The sultan demanded extravagant gifts in honor of the engagement, and without a shadow of a doubt, Liman spent his entire fortune in less time than it took to acquire. He even sold his small boats and his lands, but as yet nothing had been settled. The father stalled for time and still the wedding did not take place. In the end, Liman was refused the hand of the beautiful princess and as was the custom of the country, the sultan kept in his possession all the gifts that had been received. Thus the young ship owner found himself ruined. He therefore decided take himself to distant parts and live far from the beautiful princess. But his elderly grandmother stopped him. "Listen," she said, "in this life, the greatest wisdom lies in going without a regret from sumptuous wealth to poverty. At his death, your grandfather entrusted to me an old cap well worn with age: perhaps it can help you. This cap will allow you to go anywhere, unseen, as long as it is on your head!" And with that she pulled the object out of an old chest and gave it to him. Putting it on his head, Liman set out at once for the sultan's palace in the hope of returning with all his possessions. He slipped past the guards unseen, went through several corridors and found himself in the princess' chamber. At the sight of the beautiful princess, he took off his cap. Quickly vanquishing her astonishment and fright, Gada received him politely and plied him with questions, which the artless Liman answered, giving away his secret. Then Gada had him served a soporific drink and in a few moments, Liman fell into a deep sleep. The princess seized his magic cap and ordered her servants to throw the visitor out, over the palace wall.

When Liman regained consciousness, he found himself on the dirt path, stripped of his precious cap. Sheepishly, he returned to his hut and related the sad misadventure. His kindly grandmother comforted him and handed him a purse: "Here," she said, "try to extricate yourself from your predicament with this purse. All you have to do is put a single coin in it in order to have the same again, as many times as you wish." Liman put the magic purse to the test right away. Without a moment's delay, he set off for Goulfei palace, where, after distributing handsome gifts to one and all, he secured the collaboration of some guards who took him to Gada. Gada received him eagerly, doing her best to put him at ease, mostly, it must be averred, to make him forget the mean trick she had played on him. She even attempted to distract him by singing a beautiful love song:

LIMAN, you are the handsomest man in the world!
In strength, in riches or in marvelous deeds
In all of Chad you have no rival.
Your heart is all bravery, all magnanimity!
Your sublime virtues
Are legendary.
You have been immortalized!
Ah! if only my adoring heart
Might share in your destiny!

Flattered and seduced, Liman set down all the coins he had at the feet of the charming princess Gada. Then, so as to further win the young lady's admiration, he told her the secret of his magic purse and once again, after having him put to sleep, Gada seized his purse and threw him out into the street.

Liman now returned home without his cap or his purse. Not in the least dismayed, his kindly grandmother gave him a little cane: "This is all I have left. It has the power to transport you from one place to another, but take care, Liman, give it to no one, or you will be ruined!" Liman took the cane and made his wish: to be at princess Gada's side! No sooner said than done! In an instant he found himself in the midst of the lavish Goulfei palace. There was the princess, in full possession of her resplendent beauty. Unable to resist her bewitching charm, the young man confided his final secret. The ingenious Gada cajoled him so much and so skillfully that she was able to take the cane right out of his hands. Then she made her wish - to banish Liman to the Isle of Miseries - and in the twinkling of an eye. the ship owner found himself on a deserted island, the whereabouts of which remain unknown to this day. The Isle of Miseries is a mountain two thousand times taller than all the mountains on the earth put together. An endless sea washes at the foot of it. On its peak, lost up in the clouds, two date palms are all that grow.

In this most desolate of places, Liman wept for many days. One morning, overcome with hunger, he went to pick some dates from the first palm tree that came to hand. No sooner had he eaten them than he discovered he had grown two zebu's horns. Stricken with despair, Liman began to regret that he had not heeded his grandmother's advice. He lamented his fate and began to curse the beautiful princess. Day after day passed in this way. All hope had vanished for Liman. Exhausted and gnawed by hunger, he knew he would have to eat, whatever the cost, if he wanted to live. So he went to the second palm tree to pick dates. No sooner had he eaten them than his horns disappeared. Miraculous! The remedy had been found. Liman now ate as much of the horn-producing fruit as of the opposite fruit. That night he fell into a deep and peaceful sleep. His sleep was disturbed, however, by a great tremor in the night, which shook him abruptly awake, even as it shook the whole accursed island. In the darkness he saw a strange, massive form, as tall as a tower, furiously flapping its wings in the date palms. It was a monster, half animal, half bird. Terrified, Liman tried to make himself very tiny in his effort to hide. In the midst of his fright, however, a glimmer of hope crossed his mind. He would have to attempt the most daring feat of his life. Summoning all his courage, he approached the monster and stole quietly under its plumage. The monster felt nothing. A few moments later, it took wing and soared. Holding on ever more tightly, the young man looked down from time to time toward the earth. The monster flew for a very long time through the night. Toward daybreak, Liman spotted lights on the earth, then, letting go, he tumbled down into the void. Fate, still merciful, spared him a fatal fall. Liman landed on a thatched roof. An old woman, coming out of the hut, which was about to collapse under his weight, saw a man, half dead, whom she recognized immediately: her grandson. Filled with joy, she lifted him up and carried him to the fireside. Thanks to the attention and care of his kindly grandmother, Liman recovered his health in a few weeks.

When he had regained his strength, the young man remembered that he had brought back some of both kinds of dates in the pleat of his trousers. Disguising himself as an itinerant merchant, he went to sell his produce in the streets of Goulfei. Since dates were a rarity there, princess Gada, who was as fond of sweet things as she was of playing mischievous tricks, bought all the horn-producing dates.

The following day a rumor reverberated across the country. Everywhere, in the streets, in the houses, it was whispered that the sultan, his military adviser, the queen and the princess each had grown two zebu's horns. The news spread consternation and confusion throughout all quarters. The most eminent witchdoctors, the fetish doctors of renown and all the scholars of the occult sciences were brought, as if to a fair, to compete with one another in skill and talent. But all their collective knowledge could cure neither king, queen, nor princess. They had reached the depths of despair when young Liman appeared. He promised to cure the king who, in return, solemnly vowed to give him anything in his kingdom. Liman had the king eat a few dates and immediately his horns disappeared. The crowd was filled with admiration and wonder. In like manner he cured the king's military adviser and the queen. As for the princess, he said to her "You have taken advantage of the respect and love I have for you. Nevertheless, I forgive all the nasty tricks you have played because I still love you. I will remove your horns on one condition, that you return my magic purse, my magic cap and my magic cane."

The princess needed no coaxing: forthwith she returned the articles to their owner. Then Liman gave her the dates that were left and the horns which had made the princess quite ugly, vanished.

The onlookers cheered the young ship owner enthusiastically and the king granted him his daughter's hand. They were joined together in marriage from that day forward. The whole country joined in the joy of the wedding celebration. The beautiful princess deeply regretted her mean tricks and loved her husband tenderly. Thus the couple passed many happy days amidst the gold and silk of the magnificent Goulfei palace.

It is said that they continue to love one another somewhere in this old world of ours.

SEVEN

GAMAR AND GUIMERIE

In days of yore, lost in the mists of time, in the fertile and bustling valley of Bahr-Salamat, there lived an honorable family. It comprised the father, the mother and two fraternal twins, Gamar and Guimerie. Their entire family wealth consisted of one plump dairy cow which the two children led to pasture every day on the grassy riverbanks.

Returning home one evening, the two siblings found their mother in bed. Pale and groaning, she had a raging fever and burning temples. The two children were petrified with fear; a torturing anguish they had never before known gripped their hearts. Their mother was dying. Every passing moment, life was slipping away from her. In the throes of her agony, the poor woman sat up on her straw mat, sent for the cow, and in the presence of her two children, spoke to the animal: "Noble cow, companion of my youth, I entrust my children to you, for look, my strength is failing, my eyes are growing dim; soon I will no longer be of this world! From this day forward you will be like a mother to them, so that when I am gone Gamar and Guimerie may never know the pangs of hunger and thirst. Farewell, noble cow!" Then the flame of life flickered and their mother passed quietly away.

Several months later, Gamar and Guimerie's father remarried a widow who, like him, had been left with two children on her hands. She was a cruel stepmother to the twins, making them do the most difficult household chores and half starving them.

During the cold rainy seasons, Gamar and Guimerie had nothing but an old frayed loincloth, while the other children slept under a thick homespun blanket of camel's hair. Very early, before daybreak, at that hour when a few stars are still twinkling in the sky, their cruel stepmother would waken them brusquely, send them out to fetch water and then take the cow to pasture. Gamar and Guimerie obeyed meekly, but as soon as they reached the wide-open plain, all tinged with dew, they would weep inconsolably at the memory of their kind and gentle mother.

Lying on the grass not far away, the animal seemed to share their grief. Her wistful, ruminative eyes never left the two children. At sunrise and when the siblings felt hungry, the cow would offer them her udder and out would flow by turns milk, honey and all sorts of good things, unknown to men. The children relished them heartily. As soon as they had eaten their fill, the animal would remove her breasts and wander away to graze peaceably on the green grass.

Thus it was, that in spite of all the ill-treatment, Gamar and Guimerie always looked healthy, had a good complexion and plump cheeks, while their stepmother's children grew scrawnier and uglier by the day. Perplexed, the heartless woman sent her children to spy on them in the bush. One fine morning, her son followed the two siblings with stealth and witnessed the touching scene. Without delay, he ran to his mother, who wickedly suggested to her husband that he kill the cow, because, as she claimed, a plague was ravaging the cattle in the neighboring village. Foolish as this talk was, the man was taken in and promptly had the animal slaughtered.

Gamar and Guimerie were comfortless, overcome with grief, in despair! Without hope and now a bleak future! Without their mother and without their cow, they will now drink from the bitter cup of life. But their heartless stepmother was not content to stop there; she urged her husband to chase them from the house. Unable to withstand her selfish suggestions, one fine day their poor father led his children out into the wilds and returned home without them.

Abandoned in the bush, Gamar and Guimerie wept and cried out for help, but only their echo answered. Weary, they sat down under the shade of a tamarind tree. Tears still rolling down her cheeks, Guimerie began to play, digging her finger into the earth. In this way she discovered a trickle of water and little edible, bulbous roots which she showed to Gamar. He realized that there must be guinea fowl in the area and immediately cut down a branch to make a snare, which he set close by. Gamar was not mistaken. A few moments later a flock of guinea fowl landed there and he killed two of them. What a blessing! Sister and brother made a fire by rubbing two pieces of wood together, then roasted the birds and ate them. Afterwards they drank the clear, pure, water that flowed between the stones.

Toward evening, Gamar built a hut with some branches. All night long the children trembled as they listened to the rushing of the wind through the forest and the howling of the wild beasts. The following day, sunrise dispelled the darkness along with the children's fear. Brother and sister then emerged from their shelter and looked for ways to busy themselves. While Gamar built traps to catch does, Guimerie fashioned little earthen jars for cooling water. That day Gamar caught only one guinea fowl.

Then they had to spend another night. Lying on the pile of grass which they used as a mat, the two children didn't dare move in their sleep. Their hearts pounded; terror chilled their blood. Unknown footsteps come close, and passed by. The owl let out his lugubrious screech, the hyena her mocking laugh, the snakes their penetrating hiss, and the wind rushed menacingly through the branches.

Morning was a long time coming. At length, the chirping of the birds announced the dawn. Sleepily, Gamar and Guimerie rubbed their eyes and came out of their shelter. But what did they see? At the place where they had set their trap the day before, stood a strange creature, half doe, half human, with the face of a pretty woman, immobilized in the snare.

The monster looked at the children and called out for help. A chill of fright passed through every limb; they froze. Again the monster entreated them to help, promising all kinds of riches. Mustering all her courage, Guimerie said to the monster: "First show us these riches, give them to us; then we will set you free."

The monster cupped her hand to her mouth, let out a cry and a whole herd of cows issued forth from the unknown creature. A second cry brought forth flocks of sheep, droves of horses, camels, mules and donkeys, followed by people bearing extravagant treasures. "Now set me free," said the prisoner "and all of this will be yours." Immediately Gamar cut the vine, which was ensnaring the monster and as fast as the wind in a tornado, she vanished into thin air.

Masters of all this wealth, the brother and sister had their slaves build a magnificent kingdom comprising a great number of cities. Palaces and gardens came out of the earth and the little stream, which had trickled between the stones, miraculously swelled, rumbled, and burst its banks so that a wide river now flowed along a bed of golden sand through a jade-green plain.

Over this place of natural grandeur, where only yesterday Gamar and Guimerie had felt their hearts pound with terror, there now passed a wave of exuberant joy. The forest had given place to their kingdom, whose fame spread to the four corners of the universe. Great kings, those of Bagirmi, Wadai, Kanem, Darfur... paid them a visit and asked for their suzerainty.

Thus the brother and sister lived in sumptuous wealth. Each

year, to celebrate the founding of the kingdom, they would sacrifice hundreds of bullocks to the Divinity, host a banquet for the hungry and comfort the poor and weak. They also prayed to Allah to keep their father alive so that they might see him. God, the Merciful, granted their prayer.

One evening an old beggar appeared at the city gate. His song stirred the hearts of all who heard him and even passers-by shed tears. A little servant, having apprised Gamar and Guimerie, they invited the beggar to the palace. He arrived, limping, and began his moving chant:

Oh God, Eternal Wisdom
I am but an unworthy creature.
Kill the cow, said the cruel woman,
And I killed it.
Send the children away,
And I sent them away.
I was left on my own, and she squandered all my goods.
Then, like a tree that drops its ripened fruit,
Without a regret, she shook me off!
Since then I am without a home, without my children and
without my cow!
From door to door, from village to village, I wander
Begging for bread and confessing my sin!
Oh magnanimous passer-by, listening to my story
Do not pity me!
Harden your heart and pass by!
I am not worthy of your alms
It were better I had never been born!
Oh my cow, Oh my poor children, Oh my sweet, gentle wife!
I ask your forgiveness.
Lord, answer my prayer!

Thereupon the old man burst into bitter tears. Throughout this sad song, Gamar and Guimerie did not cease crying. Here was their father, this beggar, their father!

Without the slightest hesitation or shame, they made themselves known to him and fell at his feet, asking God to bless them and accord them happy days together, for there can be no happiness without the joy one feels in the bosom of the family.

EIGHT

THE ECLIPSE OF THE MOON

Discord and dissension exist not only among men. Up there in the heavens, the sun and the moon have vowed an unending enmity. And yet the two stars seem to be made to get along: each one is duly sublime in its plenitude: each one dispels the darkness; each one shines for man, for the animals, for the plants. Eternal wayfaring travelers, both light up the deserts, the forests, the lakes and the small valleys.

There is admittedly a difference of temperament between the two stars: whereas the sun has an intense manly vigor, that heats, energizes, and consumes, the moon has a motherly gentleness that caresses, refreshes and soothes. The star of the day is as regular as clockwork; he rises in the morning and greets nature with a burst of scarlet fire. The moon, on the other hand, lacks constancy and self-assurance; she is playful and secretive. Sometimes she appears in the west, showing only her profile, spying as it were on the world that awaits her; sometimes she shows herself in the eastern sky, boasting a radiant and full, round, white face.

But this difference of character that sets the two stars at variance still does not explain the discord that reigns between them. The cause of their enmity goes far back in the night of time.

One evening, weary of her frolicsome existence, the moon wished to meet the sun. She set out on the latter's path, climbing a treacherous slope, strewn with boulders, brambles and thorns. After having covered a considerable distance and with much difficulty, she suddenly felt faint. In the space of a few seconds, her luminous white face grew dim and a great shadow was cast over the earth. Seeing the moon approach him, the sun blew a wind which split the boulders in pieces and caused the brambles and thorns to jut out like sharp spears, thus riddling the already difficult path the moon was following with insurmountable obstacles. On top of this, he aimed his scorching rays at her and slowly the moon was consumed.

She would soon have been reduced to ashes to scatter on the earth had it not been for the men who, becoming aware of the unfolding drama, entreated the sun to desist in its destructive course of action. Banging on upturned calabashes, floating in water vessels, these families sent up to the heavens a deafening and disapproving furor. At the same time, they lit fires in front of their huts; some cooked millet, some corn, some groundnuts, and distributed the food to the young children. After they had eaten their fill, the children sent up a prayer full of innocence that reached the very depths of the heavens. Thus it was that the agonizing, celestial tragedy was averted. Overcome with pity, the sun relaxed the intensity of his rays. Gradually the moon regained her senses, got back her former strength and turned around. Resuming her planetary course, she completed her revolution around the earth.

It still happens to this day that the beautiful queen of the night repeats her tragic adventure, by entering the sun's path. And as in days gone by, the people of Chad and their children, filled with foreboding, repeat in the night a custom that is a thousand times a thousand years old, to secure the moon's deliverance and avert a cataclysmic, cosmic event which would be without precedent in the history of the world.

NINE

THE MOST BEAUTIFUL GIRL ON EARTH, HIDDEN UNDER AN ASS' SKIN

Am-Sitep was a woman as devout as she was beautiful. Thus she declined all the offers of marriage made by the many suitors in her village. To have her life better reflect her ideas and ideals, she laid out a magnificent garden around her hut. Its many birdcages attracted the blackbird with its shiny coat, the turtledove with its gray feathers speckled with crimson, the black magpie with its long tail, the yellow canary and the flycatcher which flaunts all the colors in the rainbow.

Every morning this splendid garden would open its gates to all the children in the village. Playing their various games, some would hop along the sandy paths, while others would chase one another in the shrubbery. Am-Sitep would go from one to the other, comforting those in tears and reassuring the more timid ones. And so her days were spent amidst shrieks of delight and innocent tears but when evening came and the children would go back home to their parents, Am-Sitep found herself all alone.

In the silence of the night, she would implore Allah to fill her solitude with the blessing of a child. God answered her prayer and she became pregnant. This event presented spiteful gossips the occasion to cast aspersions on her chastity and spread malicious rumors but Am-Sitep paid no heed to their slander. One morning, to everyone's great astonishment she gave birth, can you believe it, to a little ass' foal! Yes, a little ass' foal with long ears! The inhabitants of the country were filled with dismay. Men and women whispered in tones of agonizing bewilderment, some even claiming that it was surely a punishment from God. It followed that the terrified parents kept their children at home and poor Am-Sitep was abandoned by all. But far from feeling saddened, she considered herself most fortunate. Like all African mothers, she lavished affection and unremitting attention on her little ass' foal. She was never ashamed to carry her on her back and sing this little ditty:

What do you know to be more radiant that the rising sun?
My beautiful little foal!
What do you know to be sweeter than scented honey?
My graceful little foal!

As soon as she was steady on her legs, Am-Sitep let her play in the garden, where she gamboled and skipped around, letting out sonorous hee-haws! It even became her wont to leave her alone at the hut when she went out to the fields. And so it happened that one day the little ass' foal had a notion for a cake. Shutting herself up in the kitchen, she took a little maize millet and crushed it in a mortar. This commotion, when Am-Sitep was not at home, attracted the attention of an inquisitive little boy, Abakar, who was playing nearby. Succumbing to his curiosity, he peeked through the keyhole, and to his great surprise saw a beautiful little girl pounding grain. Beside her on the floor lay an ass' skin. The little boy went away quietly without breathing a word to anyone. The next day he came to find the little foal and share his cake with her. From that day forward the two became constant companions, and shared their innermost secrets.

Much later, when the day came for Abakar to choose a wife, he proposed to the foal, now a full-grown she-ass. His parents called him a fool and his friends mocked him. But Abakar was not concerned about their sneers and jeers. He had made up his mind to marry the donkey. The whole country laughed and scorned the idea. In a rage, his father took a knife and set out to kill his son but at the sight of a woman as beautiful as the dawn, the arm, about to commit the murder, dropped the weapon. Abakar simply said: "Father, meet my wife."The man could scarcely believe his eyes. He ran to embrace Am-Sitep and tell her what he had just seen. Without further ado, he went back home, invited all the villagers to the marriage banquet and served them food and drink. Then he ordered his servants to bring the most beautiful loincloths and the finest garments. "Go," he said, "dress my son and his wife. Let us rejoice in this happy union!" And in this manner, Abakar's wedding to the most beautiful girl on earth, hidden under an ass' skin was celebrated.

Am-Sitep died for joy, praising the Lord. A water lily grew on her grave, radiating white petals topped with golden stamens. This flower, symbol of the supreme beauty of woman, was the exact likeness of her daughter.

And that is why, in Chad today, the highest praise and greatest compliment one can accord a woman is to whisper softly in her ear: "You are as beautiful as Am-Sitep's daughter" or "You are as beautiful as Abakar's wife."

TEN

NIDJEMA, THE LITTLE ORPHAN GIRL

Once upon a time, there was a virtuous and trusted little girl, a good friend to all. They called her Nidjema because she was especially beautiful. Although she was an orphan, her friends knew that they could use and abuse her kindness. She would help them out of their predicaments, make up for their oversights and omissions and a fold of Nidjema's dress always concealed the best portion of her scanty dinner reserved for her friends. Now Nidjema was unhappy in her foster family, where the heaviest and most difficult chores always fell to her. It was Nidjema who fetched the water, collected the firewood, lit the fire, ground the millet and washed the calabashes, but they were never satisfied and so they would beat her.

One morning she was so badly beaten that she ran away and took off into the bush to put an end to her life. She crossed a vast wooded area without worrying about either the wild beasts or the snakes.... She had been walking for a very long time when all of a sudden, at the edge of a thicket, she found herself nose to nose with a monster which defies human conception or imagination.

Its two legs were as colossal as the thickest baobabs, its voluminous head covered with a crop of hair so profuse that birds were making their nests in it. But little Nidjema wasn't at all afraid; she simply said: "I am an orphan. My foster mother is very cruel. Never is the load of wood I gather heavy enough; never is the water I dip cool enough; never is the quantity of millet I grind large enough; the fire I light is never hot enough; the calabashes I wash are never clean enough. And so I am beaten. I've suffered so much that I have run away. On the way, I have been hungry and thirsty; the stones on my path have played havoc with my feet. I would rather die than live in this hell!"

The monster answered the little orphan: "Adorable little star! Your voice is as gentle as the breeze in the leaves. Neither the melodious song of the turtledove on a bough nor the babbling of water over rocks can match its beauty. Far be it from me to take away your life! Press on, little star...."

And Nidjema did press on, encountering again and again the same hideous creatures, each more horrible than the one before. At length, she reached the entrance to a dense area of savannah, which no one is able to locate today. As the little girl entered, huge snakes stood upright in her path but Nidjema, hastening on, did not slow down despite their painful bites. At one point, however, she fell, losing consciousness. Was this the death she so much longed for now striking her down? All we know is that when Nidjema later opened her eyes, she saw a prodigious number of vile creatures surrounding her. Giant beetles with shimmering wings, gargantuan spiders with hairy backs, poisonous centipedes and gigantic scorpions pressed against her. But, no longer afraid to die, the little girl simply said: "I am an orphan. My foster mother is very cruel. Never is the load of wood I gather heavy enough...."

As soon as she had finished speaking, a cavernous voice could be heard. Death itself answered the child: "Adorable little star! Man's destiny is inexorable. Each one awaits his hour; yours has not yet struck; so, go back to where you come from; return to your village. In this life happiness consists in being virtuous!"

No sooner were these words spoken than Nidjema found herself, as if by a miracle, transported to the side of her ever cruel, ever callous foster mother. In an instant, she regained her strength, got up and did her daily round of chores. Nidjema fetched the water and collected the firewood. After that she lit the fire, ground the millet, washed the dishes.... And then she was beaten. But the little girl remembered the cavernous voice.

All her life, it is said, she had so many virtues that it would be almost impossible to count them any more than one could count the evening stars in the azure bosom of the Chadian sky.

ELEVEN

HUNTING WITH A NET

The universe, still burning, had barely left the hands of the Eternal and already the tremendous drama of creation was unfolding. The first dawn set the sky ablaze with its ominous redness; the day broke on a savage natural world. The struggle for life was well underway; the law of the jungle prevailed. Violent instincts stirred living beings to rise up and fight one another. The deafening tumult of that day was without precedent! The earth reverberated to its innermost depths with curses and insults, shouts of victory, elation and pride, and desperate appeals for mercy. The woods and the mountains, shaken to the core, threw back the echo of these dissonant cries to the four corners of the earth.

In the midst of this enraged world and huddled in her scrubby lair, a doe clasped to her bosom a fragile and delicate fawn. Anxious and confused, she awaited the arrival of calm, tranquility, and peace, but, alas, this was not to be! Suddenly she became aware of strange whispers coming close and tall shadows surrounding her. Sensing danger, she stood up straight and rigid. Then, drawing a deep breath, she sprinted with swift, graceful agility toward the far horizon of the savannah. Now at that precise moment other tall figures rushed towards her, blocking the path. Turning around, the animal headed for the opposite side of the savannah but once again men appeared out of nowhere with their treacherous intent. Uttering loud cries, they brandished their assegais and their hunting knives. The poor doe galloped so fast that she felt neither the jabbing of the rocks nor the pricking of the thorns along her way. For a moment she thought she had cleared danger, when suddenly a huge net descended, stopping her abruptly and forever in her flight for dear life. Immobilized in the net, she let out a heart-rending wail but her cry of distress was drowned in the general din.

With raucous voices, the hunters were already crowing their victory and thinking of the share that would fall to each one, when the doe, with an almighty start, stood up tall and spoke these words: "Humans, let me live! I have a baby to nurse, do not deprive him of a mother's tenderness."

"Huh!" replied one of the hunters, "feelings are dangerous snares; they are like the glue that catches flies. Now we are not flies and the doe's words are even less like glue!" Finding this a witty speech, his companions burst into guffaws. The helpless animal made this further appeal: "Give me just a few moments of freedom, to see my little fawn one last time. I will return, I give you my word!"

"You will never trick us!" exclaimed the hunters in unison. With these words they prepared to kill her, when, all of a sudden the heavens burst into a crashing thunder. It was terrible! Unspeakable! A dazzling light coming out of the clouds, wound and spiraled its way down through space, then took the form of a man. It was the angel Gabriel, God's messenger! "Humans," he said to the hunters, "this doe is not lying. She does have a baby to nurse; grant her request; let her see her fawn one last time, I guarantee her return." The angel pled her case in a flight of divine oratory but the hunters, with their hearts of stone, would hear none of it. So Gabriel surrendered himself, taking the animal's place in the net. This was the price paid that the doe might return to her lair. After suckling her little one, she licked him all over, nuzzled him playfully, then left him forever, glancing back fondly one last time. When she got back to the hunters, she took the angel's place in the net and with courage and dignity allowed herself to be killed forthwith.

Her warm blood overspread the parched and shuddering earth, as if to lend an even more accusatory hue to the disturbing red sky of the first dawn.

Distraught by so much cruelty and lack of compassion, the angel quietly took his distance, cursing the hunters.

And that is why, in Chad, it is generally considered taboo to hunt with a net, for it is deemed neither heroic nor just.

TWELVE

THE LION'S JUSTICE

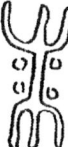

In those days, a cordial understanding reigned among the animals. Even the lion was not the fierce tyrant who today sows terror in the bush. Although feared, he was affable and readily kept company with the other animals. But among them all he particularly liked the hyena, for she was, it seemed, smarter than all the rest. For this reason he set up a company with her, to which each one brought the assets he owned: the lion brought a bull, the hyena a cow. And the responsibility of managing the shared wealth fell to the hyena. She attended to it with great diligence, to such an extent that one day, giving account of her management to her business partner, she let him know that her cow had brought a calf into the world. Immediately the lion disputed this way of seeing things. He held that, as sure as iron is hard, the calf could only have come from the bull and not from the cow. A lively exchange ensued between the partners.

"I am convinced," said the lion, "that the calf belongs to my bull, for only the bull has the power to procreate."

"I swear by all the gods the calf came out of my cow's entrails," replied the hyena.

"I won't listen to such foolishness," retorted the lion. "The calf belongs to my bull; there are no whys and wherefores, that's just how it is!"

But since the hyena persisted in taking the opposite view, the lion convened all the animals to deliver justice. The assembled animals constituted a Special Court of Law. The lion outlined the nature of his disagreement with the hyena and asked each of them to give judgment.

The elephant spoke first. Pretending to think, he shook his unsightly trunk and pronounced his judgment: "In my opinion only the bull has the power to procreate."

One after the other, the rhinoceros and the hippopotamus, raising their pachydermal mass, merely seconded what had just been said.

Next the giraffe, sweeping the sky with her long, long neck as if she sought an opinion free from all constraint, asserted with solemnity that the calf could only have been born to the bull.

The water-buffalo of timid air, the panther with his absent and devious look, the warthog with his hideous snout all corroborated with more subtlety and sophistry, the validity of this opinion: only the bull is capable of procreating, the calf could only have issued from him. After all the other animals had spoken to this effect, they noticed that the hare had not given his opinion. Summoned forthwith by the lion, the hare arrived, looking dispirited and dejected, his long ears hanging down. After acquainting himself with the nature of the lion's dispute with the hyena, the hare replied:

"Neither my physical state nor my clarity of mind permits me to put forward a well thought through and fair opinion, for I have just received some devastating news. My father who lives very far away has just given birth to a little leveret and is in great distress. I am anxious to go and care for him as his condition requires."

"Little imbecile," growled the lion, "since when have you seen a male give birth?"

"Sire," retorted the hare, "don't try to make others say what they do not believe. You have just settled the lawsuit, which sets you against the hyena. Even if the bull has the power to procreate, the calf could only have issued from the cow. The hyena has won the case." With these words, the hare took to his great legs and bounded off. Incensed, the lion leapt after him. As for the other animals, they dispersed to the four corners of the earth.

Since that day the animals have abandoned forever the custom of coming together to deliver justice. Each one has rediscovered the freedom to judge for himself what is true and fair, for on this earth, the law of the strongest prevails. The weak are always wrong and the judges, always convinced, sentence them in the name of a very vague word, justice, masquerading under a smile.

THIRTEEN

THE ADVENTURER

Beyond the town of Moundou, which means "straw," or, in the
Gambaye tongue "bondou" and extending for ten leagues around
is Doba, the capital city of the M'Baye, the Gor, the Madjingaye,
the Daye, the Kaba, the Goulaye and all the Sara peoples of Chad,
who live together in peaceful accord.

But a few kilometers from Doba, in an idyllic part of the country,
live the Sara Gor in particular. Bodo is their capital. There is an
immense forest there, where human life made its first appearance
in the world. Our forefathers still sleep on this parcel of ground.
This forest created an impassable enclosure; anyone could enter,
but never, ever could anyone leave unless he was Sara Gor. It was
a forest in its prime: trees and grasses gave way to other vegetation,
then to other grassy stretches. When the wind blew everything
crackled, stirred, exuded into nature a thousand and one perfumes.
The deeper one ventured into the Bodo forest, the more threatening
it became; at its core was a tangle of plants and a teeming profusion
of wild animals. Antelope, giraffe and gazelle ran here and there;
elephant, lion and panther loomed at every turn. Birds of every

plume glided overhead: the sparrow-hawk, the vulture, the crow, the toucan and the crane with his crown could be seen there....

In this forest, at once impenetrable, formidable and enchanting, the word "gor" meaning "encircled," "isolated," made its appearance in the Sara language. And this is the right word, for the inhabitants of the gor country, cut off from the other Sara peoples, have in their isolation evolved a language, which bears little resemblance to the Sara tongue. The history of the Sara Gor people can be traced back to this mysterious and blessed part of the country. It is said that they actually believe their race to be indigenous, that is to say, born right here. They claim to be descended from a common ancestor, whose name no one has ever known. Nevertheless, it seems certain, as certain as there is such a thing as certainty, that the descendant of this ancestor was Ngardinga. After him came M'Bainakoum, Baitokon, Assede, Mitta, Millaro and Doualet, whose impressive epic still haunts the mind.

One day, weary of living continuously in the closed circle of the Bodo forest, Millaro decided to seize his freedom. A man of imposing stature and muscularity, his agility was as daunting as his might. A man at once energetic, strong and fearless, his qualities inspired other men in the country to accompany him. So Millaro left the Bodo forest and ventured out to other places, followed by those who had confidence in him. At that time there were neither paths, tracks nor roads but this did not hinder Millaro, who ordered his followers to cut down the bush. And so it was that one could finally penetrate the forest. Seeing his people overcome with fatigue, Millaro gave the order to stop right in the middle of the bush. The place was hardly conducive to raising and educating the race. Nevertheless everyone obeyed. The location of this first settlement is no longer known to us today but the fact remains that several decades later his son, Doualet, must have left this settlement to venture further into nature's vast unknown. He founded the city of Doba on the banks of a river, whose cool, foaming torrents roared in steep rapids, thus opening up new horizons to the Sara Gor. Doualet's descendants are today known by the names M'Bailao and Mamadou Eloi. But Millaro was their ancestor and Millaro means "the one who opened the way," that is to say, the Adventurer-warrior.

FOURTEEN

THE MISANTHROPIC KING

As far back in time as men can remember, albeit they forget very fast, the oral tradition is there to remind them constantly of events that happened before they were born. Its elasticity and capacity for changing and evolving allows the tradition to yield to the exigencies of the moment; it adapts according to the place and the time in which the individuals live. And thus it guarantees the orderly continuation of custom, linking the past to the present and the present to the future. For this reason also the story of young King Choua is still told today.

At a time beyond memory, this young prince of Kanem was called to rule over a great number of subjects at the place where the town of Mao stands today. Generations of sultans had left him a legacy which retained the imprint of their collective endeavors and achievements. Choua had therefore only to put forth the effort necessary to perpetuate this tradition, already firmly established in the beliefs, ideas and customs of the people. Choua had only to follow in his father's footsteps, in his rights as well as his duties. He had only to reign, upholding the reputation, honor and valor of a dynasty and maintaining the power acquired by a kingdom over preceding centuries.

Now this was not young Choua's wish. After reigning only several months he was scandalized by the intrigues plotted and played out by the viziers, the palace officials and the state dignitaries. Most of all he was alarmed by the malicious gossips, informers and slanderers looking for a bribe. He had a particular aversion to the spiteful insinuations the men in his entourage were wont to make simply to avenge their rivals or enemies. To put an end to this state of affairs, as he thought, young Choua opened his gates to all the subjects in his kingdom. Instantly, his palace became a public place, frequented from morning until evening by a throng of people from all walks of life. He wanted to speak to everyone and listen to everyone. The lowliest citizen, mingling with the leading men in his noble dwelling, engaged him in hearty and frank conversation. But even here Choua observed that nothing could control the swirl of ambition. Pressed one against the other, outwardly content but inwardly agitated by their private passions, men would come and go, complaining of their lot in life.

More than one tried to arouse the king's pity over his lot by first speaking evil of his neighbor, then soliciting persistently for favors. Even during festivals, neither the luster of the lights, nor the beauty of things, nor even the excellence of art prevented the buzzing and busybody activity of this throng seeking favors. The more each one considered the king a personal acquaintance, the more he asked him to grant privileges at the expense of the next person. In the end, no longer knowing who should be rewarded and who should lose out, the young king decided to renounce the throne.

One morning Choua summoned his people: "My conscience forbids me from reigning," he told them. "I have resolved to extinguish in one moment a glorious past and centuries of history. Up to the present, the crown of Kanem has been hereditary. I solemnly revoke this custom and ask you, my people, to govern yourselves as you see fit. I beg you to drop your ambitions and your vain pursuits and to appoint in my place a citizen who can make you happy. I command that my wish be done. My decision is irrevocable!"

Thereupon, young Choua selected the leading men to organize the elections and stood down. That very day he left the country to go and live far from men and their intrigues.

Arriving in the heart of the bush, he built a straw hut at the foot of a large baobab whose branches equaled in girth the earth's largest trees. There he led a peaceful life among the animals whose habits he learned with each passing day. Thus he realized that men had always exaggerated the courage and ferocity of the lion and that they had underestimated the elephant's prodigious strength and gentle majesty. He observed that they had foolishly ridiculed the hyena's cowardice, the rhinoceros' clumsiness, seriousness and intelligence and the ostrich's stupidity and timidity. By the same token, men had not fully appreciated the light, graceful and airy shape of the antelope or the peculiar elegant beauty of the giraffe. Among the insects, young Choua singled out those which exhibited the most remarkable characteristics, notably the termites which cover entire plains with their conical dwellings. He determined that the locusts and the ants are quite formidable but that they are nonetheless not to be so much feared as men. Indeed, the human being has no more implacable enemy than his own kind. Human society has lost its original simplicity without gaining the slightest idea of order and morality. Deception and violence are part of the social system and men tremble constantly before men. Superstition, tyranny, anarchy, lying, cheating for the purpose of advancement and the conflicting interests of individuals, families and groups create an almost perpetual state of strife.

While the young king spent his life in the solitude of the bush observing the animals, comparing them to men and reflecting on their behavior, his people had already elected, though not without difficulty, another king. After successive compromises, the leading men and those who had some influence came to an agreement on the election of new king. They entrusted power to a former slave from Bornu, whose upbringing and cunning, reinforced by long experience of life acquired in servitude, allowed him to solicit the people's votes. Thus elevated to the highest office of the Kanembu state, the former slave was able to win over the farmers, the peasants, the cattle-herders, the pillaging Kreda people and many nobles who had inherited heavy debts. To some he made fantabulous promises: equal rights and responsibilities, agrarian reforms, redistribution of lands, revival of the economy, an improved standard of living; to others, he solemnly promised to grant privileges, extolling their noble blood and their fine business acumen. This demagoguery stirred the crowd's passionate admiration. Everyone began to praise the accession of the new king. It even happened that a few distinguished lords of the most noble traditions of the country became advocates of the new doctrine.

Transformed into professional flatterers, they sang extravagant praises to their new overlord, which earned them generous rewards at the expense of the poor. This one and that one were placed in the highest administrative posts; some became viziers and palace attendants, others became ministers and bodyguards. Not one, however, was yet satisfied with his lot and each began to malign the other to the king. Taking advantage of this underhanded rivalry, the king placed his relatives and allies, one by one, in all the key positions in the kingdom. He made them governors, state dignitaries, envoys and ambassadors. This new aristocracy became so influential that they had parliament pass a law, raising the new ruler to the ranks of the gods. Henceforth all the ancestral beliefs were not only disparaged but declared vulgar, archaic and irrational. They were replaced by a new religion which had its own pontiffs, priests, church officials, eulogists, chorus masters and lavish rituals. The citizens of Kanem were compelled to worship the ruler of the moment. An overbearing and oppressive police force assumed the right to control the behavior and the speech of individuals; people were required to repeat an incantation morning and evening, by which the monarch was supposed to pour out his blessing and his grace on their souls. Fetters and chains fell on religious freedom and free thought. This vulgar farce profoundly weakened the moral, familial and social traditions to such an extent that absurdity replaced reason and intelligence was put to sleep under the anesthetic of a despicable propaganda.

Still turning the situation to his own purposes, the new king had himself declared the supreme god and idol. On top of this, he made the people pay for the education of his children, those already born and those yet unborn, as well as for the upbringing of the children born to his supporters and in his household. In addition, he skillfully drained off Kanem's wealth to his native country. With the heavy taxes imposed on an unfortunate people at prayer, he built sumptuous palaces and magnificent showcase villas, and all this time poverty gradually consumed the country until the day when its economy, wealth and productive energy were all but exhausted. Then the new king resorted to a policy of divide and rule. He declared and had it repeated incessantly by his supporters that the people of Kanem were divided into two distinct classes, having diametrically opposed interests: on the one side there was the race of nobles and on the other the wretched mob of peasants and tradesmen. The former, rich owners of cattle and proslavers by tradition, lived off the work of the latter whom they disdained. This notion was artfully maintained with such a nasty mix of skill and persistence that it pitted the two groups of citizens against each other. The one group felt deprived of their dignity, the other felt guilt-ridden. Unrest flared up here and there, putting the country to fire and the sword. This fratricidal war was again skillfully exploited by a few men who remained faithful to their master's regime. Suddenly they showed to the people the soul of a poet and a moralist in their appeal to one and all to rally round the new king, whom they presented as the light and life of Kanem. But despite their ignorance, the people would have none of it. Their long-established practice of solidarity, as much familial and tribal as patriotic, made them unite in self defense. In a surge of cohesion, the people rose as one, demanding more justice, insisting on the cessation of famine, poverty, destitution, ill-health, illiteracy and an end to the exploitation of the public credulity for the gain of one man and his entourage. In the villages and towns of Kanem, the masses became agitated and threatening: they demanded that hereditary kingship be restored so they might recover the familial and social traditions, the foundation of Kanembu society since time immemorial. Nothing could withstand this impulse, at once conservative and revolutionary. All those who had gained from the regime now rallied to the people's cause so that they might one day be able to plead mitigating circumstances to their treachery. As for the new monarch, he took all possible steps to find a few more accomplices, who helped him flee the country one evening, disguised as a milkmaid, carrying a jar on her head. The members of his family also disappeared miraculously, absconding with what they had amassed at the expense of the Kanembu people. And so it was that the next day Kanem was at odds with itself. The revolution was henceforth without cause but that did not prevent the citizens from fighting among themselves to root out the evils of lying, enmity and hatred that had been deliberately injected into the social fabric of the country. The worst would yet have taken place had not a few wise men sent messengers to King Choua, who succeeded in bringing him out of his solitude and who, in spite of his great distrust for mankind, returned to Mao. The country was economically ruined by poverty and the vermin of corruption, but he agreed to resume power in order to restore unity, magnificence and the splendor of the nation's past prestige. In this undertaking, he was able to include all his subjects according to their various abilities and talents. Thus Kanem regained its former moral, social and economic health. Decades of interregnum had neither tarnished nor obliterated centuries of history as young Choua had wished.

The history of a people is indeed unbroken; it cannot be distorted, it cannot be truncated, much less extinguished, by an ill-conceived act or by a policy tending to the cult of personality. It constitutes the only guarantee of a people's progress.